DORA and Friends

# Welcome to Fairy World!

Adapted by Mary Tillworth

Based on the teleplay "S'more Camping" by Chris Gifford

Illustrated by David Aikins

A Random House PICTUREBACK® Book

Random House 🏠 New York

randomhousekids.com
ISBN 978-0-553-52119-1
MANUFACTURED IN CHINA
10 9 8 7 6 5 4 3 2 1
Glitter effects and production: Red Bird Publishing Ltd., U.K.

**O**ne starry evening, Dora and her friends gathered around a campfire to make s'mores—a treat made of graham crackers, roasted marshmallows, and melted chocolate. Alana had never had s'mores, and she was excited to try one.

But when Pablo opened the marshmallow bag,
he saw that all the marshmallows were gone!
*"¡Mira!"* cried Alana. Fireflies were carrying
the marshmallows away!

Kate and Emma stayed at the campsite. Everyone else chased the fireflies into a magical forest, where they turned into fairies!

"Let's follow the fairies and get our marshmallows back!" said Dora.

She and her friends followed the fairies into a cave.

Inside the cave, Pablo used a net to catch one of the fairies. "Will you help us find the other fairies so we can get our marshmallows?" he asked.
The fairy nodded. "I promise!"

The fairy introduced herself as Pinenut. She led Dora and her friends to the top of a mountain, where other fairies were throwing the marshmallows to a hungry dragon. The dragon was roasting the marshmallows with his fiery breath and gobbling them up!

Pinenut said that the dragon protected the fairies from mean goblins called *los duendes* who tried to stop them from granting wishes. In return, the fairies fed the dragon.

"*El dragón* only eats marshmallows," explained Pinenut.

Dora shook her head. "It's not good for him to eat only marshmallows!"

"But he loves them!" said Pinenut.

Just then, three dark shapes appeared in the sky. *Los duendes* were coming! The dragon tried to get up, but he could only groan. He had a tummyache!

"We need to get him some good, nutritious food!" declared Dora. *"¡Rápido!"*

The friends raced to the Fairy Garden, which was full of fruits, vegetables, and nuts, as well as sweets.

"Should we bring *el dragón* candied nuts or fruit and plain nuts?" asked Dora.

"Fruit and plain nuts!" cried Alana and Naiya.

"Caramel apples or pineapples?" asked Alana.
"Pineapples!" cheered Naiya.
Pablo scratched his head. "Bubble gum or
bananas?" He smiled. "Bananas!"
The friends collected the healthy food and
raced back to the dragon.

The friends wanted to feed the dragon healthy food, but he was full from all the marshmallows!
"We've got to get the dragon moving so he can build up his appetite," said Dora.

Alana knew the perfect workout. "Flap your arms like a dragon!" she called.

"Stomp your feet with a dragon stomp. And wiggle your dragon belly!"

After that, *el dragón* felt better—and he was hungry again!

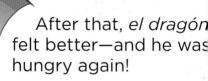

The friends fed the dragon nutritious food from the Fairy Garden. Then Pablo fed the dragon beans to help him build muscle. Now the dragon was ready to take on *los duendes*!

With a roar, the dragon rose. Using the mighty dragon strength he'd gotten from all the healthy food and exercise, he chased *los duendes* away!

Pinenut flew up to Dora and her friends. "Thank you for helping us. Now we can get back to granting wishes!" She smiled. "If you'd like to make a wish, we can make it come true!"

"I know what I want to wish for," Alana said. The friends all closed their eyes and made a wish.

When they opened their eyes, they were back at the campfire. Alana had a s'more in her hand. "It's just what I wished for!" she said happily. While she ate it, she got an idea.

A few minutes later, Alana presented her friends with a new dessert. "They're s'mores, except with fruit. I call them s'moots!"

The friends laughed as they shared Alana's delicious new treat.